Alfie's World

A Celebration

For Caroline Roberts

ALFIE'S WORLD
A BODLEY HEAD BOOK
978 0 370 32894 2
Published in Great Britain by The Bodley Head,
an imprint of Random House Children's Books

This edition published 2006

3 5 7 9 10 8 6 4

RANDOM HOUSE CHILDREN'S BOOKS
61–63 Uxbridge Road, London W5 5SA
A division of The Random House Group Ltd

RANDOM HOUSE AUSTRALIA (PTY) LTD
20 Alfred Street, Milsons Point, Sydney,
New South Wales 2061, Australia

RANDOM HOUSE NEW ZEALAND LTD
18 Poland Road, Glenfield, Auckland 10, New Zealand

RANDOM HOUSE (PTY) LTD
Endulini, 5A Jubilee Road, Parktown 2193, South Africa

THE RANDOM HOUSE GROUP Limited Reg. No. 954009
www.kidsatrandomhouse.co.uk

A CIP catalogue record for this book is available from the British Library.

Printed in China

Alfie's World

A CELEBRATION

Shirley Hughes

THE BODLEY HEAD
LONDON

HERE COMES ALFIE!

This is how Alfie made his first appearance, running home
up the street ahead of his mum, who came trundling behind
with the shopping and Annie Rose in the buggy.

Alfie is an ordinary little boy. He has a mum and a dad and a little sister called Annie Rose. He has no magical powers, and he does not go on fantastic journeys into space or anything like that. But some very exciting and interesting things happen to him all the same.

FACES, BODIES, HANDS AND FEET

Alfie has good moods and bad moods
like everybody else. This is how he
looks when he is puzzled, for instance,
or happy or cross or pleased
with himself.

Faces tell you a lot about how people are feeling. But there is plenty of expression in their bodies, arms and legs too.

ALFIE'S MUM

Alfie's mum is called
Jessica Mary. She has
reddish brown curly hair
which often gets untidy,
but Alfie likes it like that.
She sometimes gets cross
when she loses things or when
there are too many toys lying
all over the floor. But she is
extra specially good at making
up pretend games and
reading stories.

ALFIE'S DAD

Alfie's dad is called Simon. He is
good at lots of things. He can draw
funny faces and mend things that are
broken, and run with Alfie on his back.
He is not specially good at camping.
But at bed time, when Annie Rose
has gone to sleep, he and Alfie
have some great chats together.

ANNIE ROSE

Annie Rose is only just learning to talk,
but she knows how to get what she wants.
If she is in a good mood, she and Alfie play
games together. And she likes it when he
shows her the pictures in his books.

One annoying thing about Annie Rose is
that she keeps wanting to play with Alfie's
toys. One nice thing about her is that she
always thinks his jokes are funny.

Annie Rose can change from a bad mood to a
good mood very quickly!

ALFIE'S HOUSE

The house where Alfie lives stands in a row of houses which look rather the same on the outside. But inside they are all very different, and so are the people who live in them. All the houses have back gardens.

If you look hard at the picture opposite, you can see Alfie and Annie Rose playing with the hose pipe and their cat Chessie, and Mum having a nice sit-down on a garden chair. Next door, their neighbour Ron Atkinson is doing some weeding. The house next door to that is where the Santos twins, Carlos and Nico, live. They go to Parkside Primary School, where Alfie will go when he is a big boy. On the corner of the street is Mr Patel's shop, where you can buy sweets and ice creams.

ALFIE'S NEIGHBOURS

Right across the street from Alfie's house live the
MacNally family: Jean, Bob and their daughter Maureen.
Maureen is a big girl who rides around on her new
bicycle and plays the saxophone in the school
jazz band.

Maureen sometimes comes to babysit for
Alfie and Annie Rose when Mum and Dad
go out. She tells Alfie lots of interesting
things about the films she has seen and
the pop stars that she likes. Maureen is
very keen on saving the planet. This is
difficult because there are so many silly
people who throw litter about, but if
anyone can do it, Maureen can.

CATS

Alfie's family cat is called Chessie because she is
black and white, like a chessboard. She is fun to
play with when she is in a good mood, but she
runs off when Annie Rose tries to squeeze
her too hard or hang on to her tail.

For many years the MacNallys had a cat called Smoky. Everyone was very sad when he died, especially Bob. So Maureen gave him a kitten which they called Boots, because he had white paws.

Now Boots has grown into a fine, friendly cat who everyone likes except Chessie.

Boots and Chessie eye one another across the street, and if they get any closer there is sometimes a fight!

ALFIE'S TOYS

Flumbo

Alfie's special friend is his elephant, Flumbo. He was knitted by an old lady, and he is nearly as old as Alfie. One terrible day some moths were found living in Flumbo's inside stuffing. He had to be unpicked and re-stuffed, but he is feeling ever so much better (and much younger) now.

Willesden

Alfie has another stuffed toy called Willesden, who is very proud to have his name on a London bus. He is quite sure that the bus company have called the bus after him, though it was really the other way round. And it was Alfie who thought of giving him that name.

ANNIE ROSE'S TOYS

Teddy One Ear

Teddy Big

Portly Pig

Raggedy Ann

Bonny

Buttercup

Daffodil

Mr Bones

Beautiful Elizabeth

Annie Rose has a lot of toys.
She likes to have the cuddly ones in
her cot at bed time. But not Elizabeth,
her best doll, who has her own bed and a
special box for all her very pretty clothes.

Daffodil is a knitted duck and Mr Bones is a very old toy dog. They once belonged to Alfie, but he has now decided that they are rather babyish and has kindly passed them on to Annie Rose.

Annie Rose is very fond of her toys, although she sometimes throws them about. Buttercup (also known as Luvadees) is Annie Rose's most favourite toy. She often goes out with Annie Rose in the buggy, and great care has to be taken to make sure that she does not fall out or get lost.

MEET ALFIE'S FRIENDS

Bernard *Daniel* *Min* *Kate* *Sara* *Sam* *Lucille*

Alfie has lots of friends. They go to nursery school together and play at each other's houses afterwards.

Karim

Freddie

They go to one another's birthday parties too.

Annie Rose

Marian

Lily

Annie Rose's best friends are Marian and Lily.

BERNARD

Bernard is Alfie's best friend.

He is not always quiet or well behaved. His best game is pretending to be a monster or a savage animal.

He does not have any little brothers or sisters, only one big brother who goes to college. This is just as well because his mum finds Bernard quite tiring sometimes. But she is sure that one day he will grow up to have perfect manners.

Some children find Bernard a bit frightening.

But he is one of Annie Rose's favourite people. She always looks for him when he comes out of nursery school and waves her arms about when she sees him. One of the first proper words Annie Rose learned to say was "Dernard!" She thinks his gorilla imitations are wonderful.

PLAYING

Alfie and Annie Rose's best time
for playing together is in the
early morning, before Mum
and Dad wake up.

They have some good games
out in the back garden too.

Alfie's favourite
games, when he is
playing on his own,
are with his cars
and trains.

When Bernard comes
to play at Alfie's house,
Annie Rose always
wants to join in, but
they won't often
let her.

But sometimes Bernard
kindly gives her rides,
pushing her about on the
floor in a cardboard box.
That is her favourite game.

IN THE PARK

In the park, where Alfie often plays, there are plenty of big trees and lots of grass to run around on, a fountain, and a sandpit, and places to climb, and a pond with ducks. There is a statue of a very grand gentleman, sitting high up on his chair. Once upon a time he was so grand that when he went out he wore a top hat, and the whole park was his back garden. Now, there he sits, with the pigeons and ducks for company.

PETS

Alfie's very good friend the milkman
and his wife have a black and white
dog called Jacko. He was a poor
little stray puppy when the milkman
found him, and Alfie remembers
seeing him fast asleep, curled up
in a hat on the milkman's van.

Now Jacko is a grown-up dog
and he once won first prize
in a pet show.

Alfie's friend Sara has a pet goldfish, Gobbolino, who lives in a little tank of his own with weeds and shells and a plastic mermaid.

When Alfie and Annie Rose go to play with their friends Min and her little sister Lily, they are allowed to stroke their two beautiful rabbits, Bianca and Domino.

Bianca is a white rabbit with pink eyes and pink insides to her ears. Domino's eyes are brown and she has black and white fur.

GRANDMA'S HOUSE

Alfie has a grandma who lives in the country. He has lots of adventures when he is staying with her. This is a picture-map of all the places around where she lives.

Mrs Hall's cottage

To the main road ←

Jim and Lorna Gatting's house

Apple orchard

Stream where Alfie and Mum went exploring

Woods

Big rocks

Secret place where Alfie and Mum once saw a snake

Field where Alfie and Dad camped out

Jim ...tting's pig

Field where the sheep live

Grandma's pond

Field where the cows live

Grandma's house

...e and ...s pen

If you turn over, you will find the story of an exciting adventure which happened one summer when Grandma was looking after Alfie and Annie Rose.

LOOKING FOR WINNIE

Alfie's grandma lived in the country with her two cats, Juno and Belle. The cats slept in baskets in the kitchen, near the stove because they liked being warm. Just up the lane from Grandma's house lived Jim and Lorna Gatting. Their son was grown up and had gone to live far away in New Zealand. They had a dog called Shep and a pig and some hens and two pet tortoises, Winnie and Fred, who were very old. Fred was eighty-nine and nobody knew how old Winnie was; perhaps nearly a hundred, Lorna said.

In winter Winnie and Fred were sleepy and liked to be indoors in their cosy
boxes full of straw. In summertime they lived outside in the Gattings'
back garden. They had a pen with a little wooden house in it and
a grassy space with wire around it to stop them getting out.
Alfie and Annie Rose often helped to feed Winnie and Fred.
They ate bits of lettuce and tomato
and they specially liked wild
flowers called buttercups.

Alfie often collected a big
bunch of them after Jim had cut the grass.
He liked watching Winnie and Fred stretch out
their leathery necks to nip off the flowers and
slowly chew them up in their wide tortoise jaws.

One morning when Alfie and Annie Rose and Grandma went to
visit the tortoises, they found Lorna very upset. She told them
that when she went out that morning, Fred was there in the pen
as usual but Winnie was nowhere to be seen!
She was not inside the little house.
Lorna had searched in the long
grass around the pen but
there was no Winnie!

"She must have got out
somehow," said Lorna anxiously.
"She always was a bit of a
wanderer. But she can't
have gone far because
tortoises are very
slow walkers."

Alfie and Grandma and Annie Rose helped Lorna to search for Winnie. They looked all over the garden, under the bushes and around the shed.

You can't call or whistle for a tortoise like you can for a cat or dog. Anyway, Alfie had a feeling that Winnie would not have taken any notice even if she *had* heard them calling her.

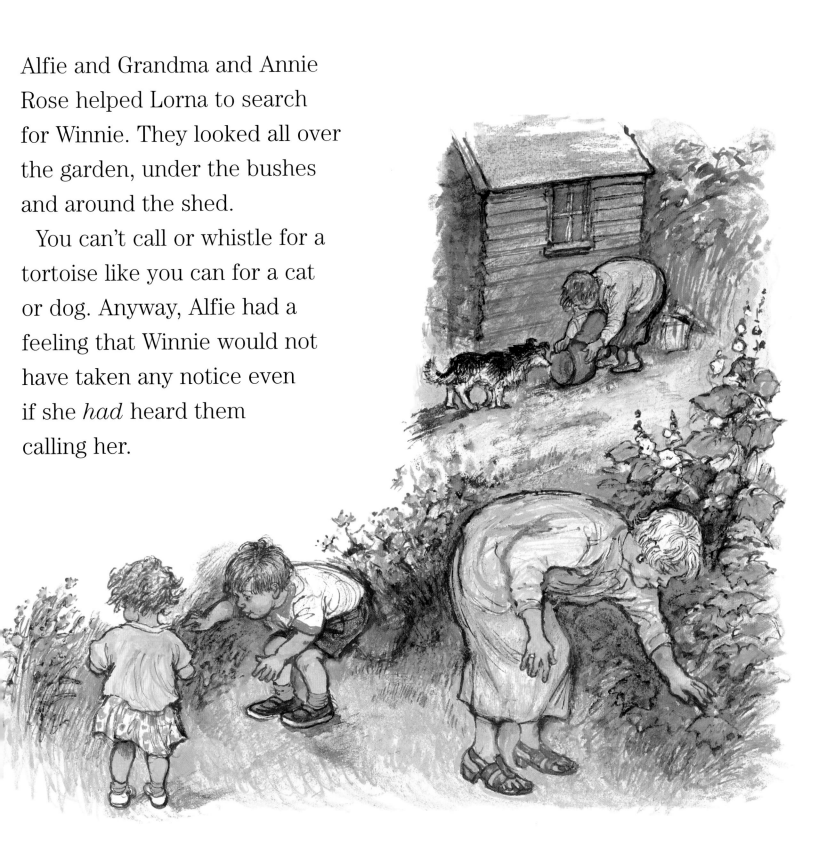

At supper time Alfie was too worried
about Winnie to eat much.

"Perhaps she fell into the pond,"
he said. "Can Winnie swim?" he
asked Grandma.

Grandma was doubtful.
"I hope she didn't get into the lane,"
she said. "I don't like to think of
her lying on her back in a
ditch. Once tortoises are on
their backs they can't get
right way up again."

At bed time it was still light and sunny. Grandma said that Alfie and Annie Rose could come with her for one last Winnie hunt. They set out up the road, looking carefully in the ditch all the way. They walked past the Gattings' house and turned into the lane where old Mrs Hall lived. Still there was no sign of Winnie. Then Grandma said that they really would have to turn back. "Winnie couldn't possibly have got this far anyway," she said.

Mrs Hall's cottage was very neat and tidy, with neat, tidy flowerbeds in her garden. Leading up to the front gate was a neat and tidy path picked out with big round stones on either side, which were painted white.

"Come on, Alfie, it's long past your bed time," said Grandma.
  But Alfie hung back. He was looking very hard
at Mrs Hall's stones. He noticed that one
of them was not white but brown.
He ran over to get a closer look,
and then he saw that it
was not a stone at all,
it was Winnie!

"Well spotted, Alfie!" said
Grandma, giving him a hug.
"I never imagined that
Winnie could walk so far.
Tortoises can't be such
slow walkers after all."

Alfie picked up Winnie and carried her carefully
back to the Gattings' house. Lorna was delighted.
She just could not stop saying how clever Alfie was
to have found her, and how naughty it was of Winnie
to go off like that and pretend to be a stone.

They carried Winnie into the garden and put her back in the pen. She stretched out her neck and looked about with her beady black tortoise eyes. Alfie and Annie Rose fed her with an extra supply of buttercups.

"I'm *so* glad we've got her back," said Grandma.

But Fred did not seem particularly pleased to see Winnie. He just went inside his shell and would not come out.

BONTING

One fine morning Alfie went into his back garden and found a very special stone. He put it in his pocket and he called it Bonting.

A lot of children have their own special Bonting. Some have whole collections, beautifully painted.

Some mothers find that they have a problem caused by too
many Bontings all over their kitchen floor. One little girl found
a Bonting with a perfect "M" on it in a pale white line running
through the smooth, grey stone. She gave that one to her mum.

One interesting thing about stones is their shape, and wondering how
old they are. You can find lovely Bontings everywhere. If you don't have
a garden, the park or the seaside are excellent places to look for them.

AT THE SEASIDE

This book has to end at
the seaside, on a sunny day,
when the pale green sea is
full of sparkles, and little
waves are running in across
the sand, one after another,
and sucking back the stones.
And there are sandcastles to
build, and channels to dig,
and picnics and ice creams,
and rock pools full of
exciting things to explore.
After home and Grandma's
house, the seaside is
Alfie's favourite place
in all the world.

*The illustrations for this book are taken from roughs,
sketchbooks and other original source material
which went into the creation of the Alfie books.*